This

Walker Book

belongs to:

_____

For Marion
T. L.

For Grandma
and Grandpa
R. H.

First published 2010
by Walker Books Ltd
87 Vauxhall Walk,
London SE11 5HJ

This edition published 2011

1 2 3 4 5 6 7 8 9 10

Text © 2010 Tanya Landman
Illustrations © 2010 Richard Holland

This book has been typeset in
ITC Cushing Book.

Printed in China.

British Library Cataloguing in Publication
Data: a catalogue record for this book
is available from the British Library.

ISBN 978-1-4063-3077-9

www.walker.co.uk

Mary's Penny

Written by

Tanya Landman

Illustrated by

Richard Holland

WALKER BOOKS
AND SUBSIDIARIES
LONDON • BOSTON • SYDNEY • AUCKLAND

Long, long ago –

way back in the golden, olden days –

there lived a farmer

and his three grown-up children,

Franz, Hans and Mary.

FRANZ

was brawny. His arms were as thick as branches,

and his hands were as big as paving slabs.

HANS

was beefy. His legs were as thick as tree trunks,

and his feet were the size of rowing boats.

Then there was

Mary.

Mary was neither brawny

nor beefy. Her arms and legs

were as slender as sticks.

Mary didn't say much.

But Mary had a very special,

secret something:

Mary had brains.

The farmer had a problem.

He simply couldn't decide who should run the farm

after he was dead and gone.

Should it be

FRANZ or HANS?

Should it be

HANS or FRANZ?

Franz or Hans? Hans or Franz?

All day long the names went round and round in

his head. It didn't occur to him to think of

Mary,

because this was long, long ago –

way back in the golden, olden days –

and everyone thought that girls couldn't

run farms.

franz FRANZ
HANs franz *hans*
hans *franz*

One bright morning the farmer called his sons to him.

"I have an idea," he said. "We'll have a competition.

And whoever wins the competition shall run

the farm when I'm dead and gone."

The farmer dug deep, and pulled two bright

pennies from his pocket. He handed one to

FRANZ and one to HANS.

"With your one penny, you must each buy something

that will fill the whole house."

Franz and Hans scratched their

heads and tried to think.

Mary

watched and listened, and

said nothing.

FRANZ

was first to try, and the next morning

he set off for market. He looked at apples

and pears, and milk and cheeses.

But in the end he bought a cartload of straw,

because this was long, long ago –

way back in the golden, olden days –

and you could buy an awful lot of straw

for a penny.

He piled it onto the cart, up and up until the cart

was so heavy the horse could hardly pull it.

When

FRANZ

got home, he started to fill the house with straw.

He carried and stacked, and carried

and stacked, and carried and stacked,

and the house got fuller and fuller and fuller.

He covered the floor with straw and then the pile

started to rise up the walls. He had got

halfway up the windows when he ran out.

There was no more straw left.

Franz had failed.

That night, they all had to sleep in the cattle shed.

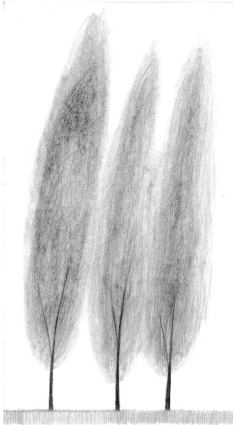

The next morning,

HANS

set off for market. He looked at apples and

pears, and milk and cheeses.

And in the end he bought a cartload of feathers,

because this was long, long ago –

way back in the golden, olden days – and you could

buy an awful lot of feathers for a penny.

He piled sackloads onto the cart, up and up until

the cart was so heavy that the horse could hardly pull it.

When he got home, he started

to fill the house with feathers.

HANS

carried and stacked and sneezed,

and carried and stacked and sneezed,

and carried and stacked and sneezed,

and the house got fuller and fuller and fuller.

He covered the floor with feathers, and then the pile

started to rise up the walls, up over the windows,

almost as high as the rafters. Almost. He had got

nearly all the way to the roof when he ran out.

There were no more feathers left.

Hans had failed.

That night, they all had to sleep

in the cattle shed again.

"WHAT AM I TO DO?"

wailed the farmer, sadly.

"WHAT AM I TO DO?

What am I to do?

What am I to do?"

Mary

watched and listened, and said…

"Where's *my* penny?"

The farmer looked at her.

"You?" spluttered the farmer. "But you're a *girl*!

Everyone knows that girls can't run farms."

"Father," said Mary quietly.

"It takes brains not brawn to run a farm.

Give me *my* penny, and I shall show you."

Slowly, reluctantly, the farmer dug deep in his pockets

and took out his very last penny.

Mary set off for market. She did not look at apples

or pears, or milk or cheeses. She did not look at straw or feathers.

Instead, she went straight to the candlemaker, and bought

a small candle and a tinderbox with which to light it.

This was long, long ago – way back in the

golden, olden days – and candles didn't cost much.

Mary had some change from her penny.

She visited the knife seller, and bought a tiny penknife.

Then she went down to the riverbank,

cut a length of hollow reed,

and sat in the warm sunshine,

working at the reed with her little knife.

When the sun began to set,

she returned home.

It was dark when she called her father

and two brothers into the farmhouse.

Mary said nothing.

She struck the tinderbox and lit the candle.

She lifted the river reed to her lips and blew,

and out came the sweetest, softest melody.

When she had finished playing, there

was a very long silence.

At last the farmer took

Mary's hand in his, and said quietly,

"Mary,

you have filled the house not once

but many times over. You have filled it with light,

and so filled it with knowledge.

You have filled it with music, and so filled it with joy.

And because you have filled the house with light

and knowledge, and music and joy,

you have also filled the house with wisdom.

You shall run the farm from

this day forward."

And even though this was long, long ago –

way back in the golden, olden days –

when everyone thought that girls

couldn't run farms …

Mary did.

And the farm prospered
and flourished.

Mary's Penny

About *Mary's Penny*, Tanya Landman writes, "I can't remember where or when I heard this traditional story for the first time, but I can clearly recall the thrilling tingle that swept through me when it drew to its magical – and perfectly right – conclusion.

At its heart lies a golden nugget of old wisdom that gleams as brightly today as it did centuries ago. Everyone – young or old, male or female – can delight in the underlying theme: a little ingenuity and a drop of creative thinking can triumph over physical strength or brute force. It's a message that's as relevant now as it ever was. But watch out for that cat – I'm sure he's up to something…"

Tanya Landman

Tanya Landman is the award-winning author of *Apache*, *The Goldsmith's Daughter* and *Waking Merlin* as well as the Poppy Fields murder mysteries, which includes *Mondays Are Murder* (winner of the Red House Book Award), *Dead Funny* and *Dying to be Famous*. Her writing has been described as captivating, striking and intelligent. *Mary's Penny* is Tanya's first picture book.

Richard Holland

Richard Holland is the stylish young illustrator of *The Museum Book* by Jan Mark and *The Time Book* by Martin Jenkins. While studying illustration at Loughborough University, Richard developed the collage technique that he uses so effectively in *Mary's Penny*.

www.walker.co.uk